Copyright © 2012 by Xavier Finkley

POOP!
There It Is

by

Xavier Finkley

My mom said she's tired
of changing my diaper.
I consider her my number one
wiper!

My dad says
"please, son go in the potty!"
When I go in my diaper,
I feel a bit naughty!

My sister says "you stink,
get out of here!"
She can't stand the smell
that comes from my rear!

Finally my dad called a
"poop intervention",
The family said they had
something to mention.

"We love you a lot, but the diapers must go!"
I clenched my fists and just hollered
"no!"

"Come on, son-we all
go in the potty."
"Your sister,
your dad
and even your
mommy!"

"Just let us know
when
you have
to go."

"We'll help you
along, we can
take it quite slow."

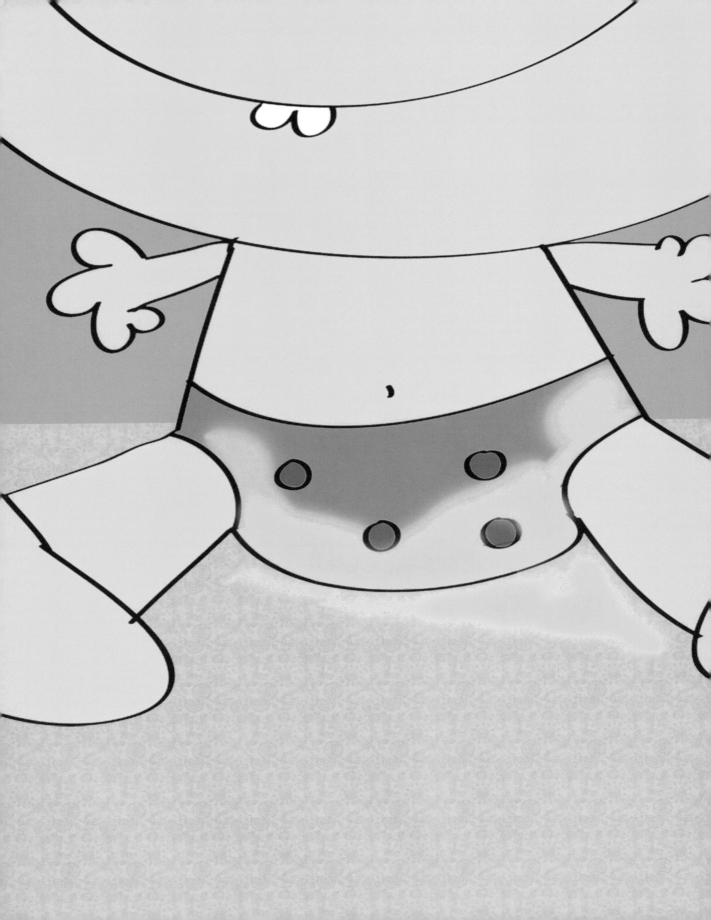

I thought about it and
finally agreed.
But my diaper was wet,
I already peed!

The poop was coming,
I had to go!
I pulled my
pants way down low.

I sat on the
top and dangled
my feet.
I inserted my seat--
it's special and neat!

After a minute,
I was all done!
I called to my family,
"come here,
quick,
run!"

"poop!

there it is! I did it dad!"
My sister and mom
were **SO** very glad!

I wiped myself clean and
flushed it all down.
For once my diaper was
no longer brown!

So big boys and girls,
now is the time.
Get rid of your diapers,
like I got rid of mine!

Made in the USA
Lexington, KY
19 June 2015